Katherine Berry di Zéréga

The Children's Paradise

Katherine Berry di Zéréga

The Children's Paradise

ISBN/EAN: 9783744791359

Printed in Europe, USA, Canada, Australia, Japan

Cover: Foto ©Andreas Hilbeck / pixelio.de

More available books at **www.hansebooks.com**

In the heart of an agèd oak
Once dwelt a bewitching fay.

THE

CHILDREN'S PARADISE

BY

KATHARINE B. ZEREGA

With Illustrations

BY

LUCY G. MORSE

NEW YORK
G. P. PUTNAM'S SONS
182 FIFTH AVENUE
1877

PREFACE.

THE simple stories told in rhyme, contained in this volume are principally founded upon facts, and were recounted originally for the benefit of the houseful of boys and girls whose performances are portrayed in the 'Children's Paradise.' Their earnest approval has emboldened the author to submit them to the public, trusting that they will meet abroad with some slight share of the favor already accorded them at home.

CONTENTS.

THE CHILDREN'S PARADISE.

THERE is an island fair and green,
 No sweeter spot was ever seen,
  Where children play
  The livelong day,
And gladly greet the sun's first ray,
This isle which to the eastward lies
Is called the Children's Paradise.

A stately mansion built of stone
In lordly grandeur stands alone
  On rising ground,
  While all around
Orchards and gardens fair abound,

The lawn slopes down on either side
To meet the coy coquettish tide.

And birds delicious songs there trill,
The air with melody they fill,
        Till one would say
        That every day,
They celebrate a feast so gay,
At which fireflies assist at night
And flood the lawn with radiance bright.

Upon a strip of shining sand
Each morn a busy blithesome band
        Display their skill
        With earnest will
By building forts and castles, till

The rising tide warns them to fly
And shelter seek in woods near by.

And now in truth begins their fun,
For, shielded from the noonday sun,
　　Such pranks they play
　　You'd really say
Their senses all had flown away;
Wildly they scale the trees and rocks,
Regardless of torn hats and frocks.

Weary at last, and grown more meek,
The poultry yard they gladly seek,
　　And fowls they feed
　　With divers seed,
Just as they've eaten all they need,
The farmer's wife protests in vain,
She cannot stop them, that is plain.

Now to the dairy each one flies,
And there secures a glorious prize,
    A brimming glass
    They quickly pass,
And gayly drain it, lad and lass,
While pans of cream so *yellow*, lo!
They leave as *blue as indigo.*

The barn they visit now with joy,
And there, each girl and romping boy
    Roll o'er and o'er
    The spacious floor,
They laugh, they scream, they shout, they roar,
And pelt each other with the hay,
While *burials* take place each day.

They scarce can spare the time to dine,
Although their appetites are fine,

The Children's Paradise.

When out again,
Adown the lane
They run with all their might and main,
To see the horses, dogs, and cows,
And watch the farmer as he ploughs.

O'er roads so charming, oft they drive,
And fill the wagon like a hive,
The coachman kind,
Time out of mind
Has loved them ; and can always find
In *any* carriage, large or small,
Room for the darlings, one and all.

But when there comes a rainy day,
These children all are forced to stay
In doors, and then
A thousand men
Make no more racket, even when

On Gold or Stock Exchange they bawl
Within a lofty frescoed hall.

They chase through corridors so wide,
Down the broad bannisters they slide,
  They skip, they prance,
  They sing, they dance,
Deafen their parents, uncles, aunts,
All of whom heave a thankful sigh,
When bed-time hour draweth nigh.

I think I'll scarcely need to tell,
For by this time you'll know it well,
  What monarchs reign
  (Scarce state maintain)
Upon this island of the main
None but *grandparents* would allow
Such escapades so oft, I trow.

And now my children ; fare you well.
Perhaps some day (no one can tell)
  If you are good,
  (That's understood)
We'll hie away to that green wood,
And you will open wide your eyes
To see the CHILDREN'S PARADISE.

SPRING *vs.* WINTER.

NOT long ago and gentle Spring
    Lay sleeping in the shade,
When o'er her charming countenance
    A wand'ring sunbeam played.

Then suddenly, she started up
    Exclaiming in surprise,
" I didn't dream it was so late,
    Dear me! how *Tempus* flies!"

" But tardy though my 'wakening be,
    I'll let old Winter know
His reign is over now, and he
    At once had better go."

" Strange stories I have heard of him
    Affecting genial ways,
  And striving to deceive mankind
    With counterfeit spring-days."

" Till mortals grown too credulous
    Duped by unwonted wiles,
  Threw off their wintry garb, that they
    Might revel in his smiles,"

" Which straightway disappeared in frowns,
    While with demoniac glee
  He scourged the shuddering earth with storms.
    And lashed the maddened sea."

" Such conduct is unworthy of
    My rough but honest friend,
  I think that I'll suggest to him
    His ways he'd better mend."

" I'll go and call upon him now,
  He don't suspect I'm near,
And armed with sunbeams sure and swift,
  His wrath I need not fear."

Her vernal robe's disordered folds
  She re-arranged with care,
And twined a wreath of violets
  Amid her golden hair.

Then over all she threw a veil
  Of softest silv'ry mist,
Through *this* disguise, she gayly cried,
" He'll never pierce, I wist."

So with a gay and lightsome mien
  She tripped to Winter's door,
And in a low, beseeching tone
  Admittance did implore.

"Come in," roared Winter, in a tone
    That had she been a mortal
Would have transformed her into stone,
    Before the frozen portal.

But fearlessly our saucy Spring,
    Entered the drear domain,
While Winter from his icy throne
    Gazed on her with disdain.

"What do you here, oh, maiden rash?"
    He cried in stern surprise,
In haste she flung the veil away
    And raised her beaming eyes,

While from their sunny gleaming depths
    Shot forth two rays of light,
Which straight transformed the gloomy hall
    Into a palace bright.

Old Winter trembled on his throne
 Before the vision gay,
Then slowly sinking 'neath her glance,
 He melted quite away.

THE DRYAD.

CLOSE, close by my window,
　　A cherry tree stands,
Its branches wave gently,
　　Like beckoning hands.
A dear little dryad
　　There dwells in this tree,
And she whispers, and whispers,
　　Sweet stories to me.

She's a gay little creature,
　　All clad in bright green,
A figure so dainty
　　There never was seen,

A rose-colored girdle
  Confines her small waist,
Dame Nature has dressed her
  In exquisite taste.

When first I beheld her,
  'Twas one summer day,
As propped by soft pillows,
  Aweary I lay,
Ah! sad seemed my destiny,
  Life, full of grief,
When turning, I saw her
  Swing forth on a leaf.

And then, in response
  To my look of surprise,
With a pitying glance
  Of her dark tender eyes,

The Dryad.

She said, " I have watched you
    For many an hour,
To solace your sorrow
    Perchance I've the power."

" Thank you kindly," said I,
    For her clear cheery voice,
Already had made
    My spirit rejoice.
" But tell me, bright being,
    Pray how came you here?
For sure you were nurtured
    In some remote sphere!"

" Earth never has moulded
    So dainty a sprite!"
But she cried, laughing gayly,
    " You've not guessed aright,

This tree and myself,
　To her owe our birth,
We were both of us nourished,
　By kind Mother Earth."

Enlightened at last,
　I cried, " Ah ! I see,
You're a dryad, and so
　Belong to the tree.
The fame of your race
　Has been chanted in story
Till a halo surrounds you
　Of mythical glory."

" But then I am certain
　The poets have told
How dryads in *oak* trees
　Lived always of old,

So you'll understand then,
It seems strange to me
To see you ensconced here
In this cherry tree."

" Some doubt your existence
For ages have flown,
Since one of your race has
Conversed with our own.
And so, little dryad,
Oh! tell me, I pray,
Why should *I*, above all
Be honored to-day?"

" I'll answer your question,"
She then made reply,
" But promise me first,
Whenever you sigh,

You'll think of my story,
　　Perhaps for awhile
'Twill lighten your sorrows,
　　And cause you to smile."

" The poets, (whom all of
　　Our race do adore),
Have rightly described us
　　As living of yore
In oak trees alone, but—
　　I'm happy to say,
With such stupid customs
　　We've done quite away."

"And know; that we never
　　Our presence reveal,
Save to do some good action,
　　Some sorrow to heal.

The Dryad.

Now many there are
    Scattered over the land,
Who our language, alas!
    Cannot understand."

" 'Twould be of no use
    Before *them* to appear,
They'd neither be able
    To see, or to hear.
That's the reason so seldom
    You ever have heard,
Of a dryad, with man
    Exchanging a word."

" We're endowed with an instinct
    Unerring and true,
As to whom we may speak,
    And I instantly knew

When I saw *your* sad face
   That you'd comprehend
My words, and would know
   They were those of a friend."

" But *now* to my story—
   You'll laugh when you hear
This morn I completed
   My *one hundredth* year.
I don't doubt you think it
   A very strange thing,
At *my* age, to be able
   To skip, dance and sing !"

" Shall I tell you the secret ?
   I banish dull Care,
No matter *what* happens
   I *never* despair.

'Tis worrying makes
    Mortal's hair turn so gray,
And from cheek and from lip
    Drives the roses away."

" Bitter thoughts wring the life
    From each healthful limb,
Plough wrinkles, and cause
    Brilliant eyes to grow dim.
Believe what I tell you,
    It is a sure sign
You'll never grow old, if
    You cease to repine."

" You're thinking perhaps,
    'Tis no merit in me
Not to murmur, when I've
    Such a home as this tree,

But within fifty years
    I've been known twice to sigh,
And once, I was tempted
    To sit down and cry."

" Twice, the sun was so hot
    It dried up each cherry,
And I *couldn't* be gay
    And light-hearted and merry,
When I thought how the birds
    And the children would mourn
The loss of the fruit,
    So I felt quite forlorn,"

" Till I thought to myself,
    How sinful to sigh !
Next summer, I'm sure
    'Twill not be so dry,

The fruit will taste better
    For such a long fast,
Oh! we will have many
    A royal repast!!"

"And just as I thought,
    It really proved so,
Next summer's sun shone
    With a less fervid glow,
The fruit in rich clusters
    Most temptingly hung;
The children rejoiced, and
    The birds gayly sung."

"Then once, Madam Redbreast,
    (Who lives on yon bough,)
Had a loss, which I can't bear
    To think of, even now.

One day not long since
    A cruel boy stole
Her nest and five eggs.
    Do you think he'd a soul?"

"Oh! how my heart ached
    For the poor little Mother!
While I helped her to build
    A nest like the other.
Now she's five pretty eggs,
    (You can see them through there)
Like me, she's determined,
    She will not despair."

"Perhaps you imagine
    I've nothing to do?
You'd change your opinion,
    If only you knew

The Dryad.

How hard I'm at work
    In bright summer weather,
Brushing bugs from the fruit,
    With a yellow-bird's feather."

"And then when the cherries
    At last disappear,
I keep the leaves fresh
    Till they're yellow and sere,
So when Winter comes on
    I am ready to rest,
Coiled up in the depths
    Of a robin's old nest."

She ceased—and to my brow
    A flush of shame arose;
As I thought how *she* had mourned,
    Only over *others'* woes.

"Thanks, thanks!" I cried, "dear dryad,
    For the lesson you have given,
'Twill nerve me for life's trials
    And lead me home to heaven."

Since then she often comes
    To cheer my weary days,
And talks with me. or sings
    Delicious roundelays.
And as fainter grow the notes
    Of some dreamy woodland air,
I gently fall asleep,
    Within my easy chair.

ONE HUNDRED DOLLARS REWARD.

THERE is a naughty little mouse
    That every single night
Scampers about our nursery floor
    And gives us many a fright.
Our nice wood-work he often gnaws,
    He stumbles and he squeaks,
And oh! I can't *begin* to tell
    The half of all his freaks.
Now Marguerite (she is our nurse)
    A trap did once prepare,
And then with nicely toasted cheese
    She furnished it with care,
Then placed it gently on the hearth,
    Thinking he'd *surely* bite.

Alas! wise mousie's movements proved,
  She did not guess aright,
For when the clouds of night dispersed
  And in the early morn,
We looked to see the poor dead mouse
  Behold! the *cheese* was gone.
There stood the trap, quite safe and sound,
  But minus was the cheese,
And mouse had walked off with his prize
  Not saying *if you please.*
Amazed we looked around the room,
  Our cheeks were pale with fear,
Then whispered softly, "can there be
  A *fairy* hidden here?
For who has ever known a *mouse*
  Do such a thing before?
But then, they say that fairies walk
  Upon this earth no more."

What can we do? pray some one tell,
  To rid our troubled house
Of this most *crafty, greedy, naughty,*
  Noisy little mouse?
We've tried all sorts of traps, but they
  Are not of any use,
So just at present there exists
  A most unwilling truce,
So a reward we offer here
  To anyone who will,
Find us a trap to catch a mouse
  That's *very hard to kill.*"

DEATH OF THE MOUSE.

(SEQUEL TO THE FOREGOING.)

"THE deed is done! oh, the deed is d
    Poor Mousie at last is caught,
That he'd never be really and truly killed,
    We *really* and *truly* thought.

Now Baby said, " he was a wise mouse,"
    And that was the reason, perhaps
For a long time he'd not once come near
    Our grand mechanical traps."

But it seems he'd only grown tired
    Of feasting on toasted cheese,
He'd eaten it often at parties,
    At *breakfasts, dinners,* and *teas.*

Then too, although we ne'er knew it,
    What he delighted in most,
I'm sure you will hardly believe it,
    Why it was *hot buttered toast.*

So his palate proved traitor to him,
    For our nurse last night, instead
Of baiting the trap with toasted cheese,
    Did substitute toasted bread.

And there in the morning we found him,
    A-lying all stark and cold,
Luckless victim to hot buttered toast,
    And now, my story is told."

THE FOREST FAIRY.

IN the heart of an aged oak
  Once dwelt a bewitching fay,
Who danced in the bright moonlight,
  And slumbered throughout the day.
Her bed was of soft thistle down,
  And her bath was a drop of dew,
Her robe was a gossamer wing,
  And a tiny shell was her shoe.
Full oft on a midsummer night,
  When high rode the silvery moon,
From the topmost branch of a tree,
  She would sing an enchanting tune,
Till the birdlings stirred in their nests,

The Forest Fairy.

And the nightingale paused to hear
A song, far surpassing her own,
   In notes so exquisitely clear.
Then swinging from bough to bough,
   She would dance round each downy nest,
And laugh at the wondering gaze
   Of blue-bird, or robin redbreast,
Oft a squirrel so swift she would mount,
   And fast through the air as she flew,
She would startle the woods far around,
   With a clear ringing hunter's halloo.

When Jack Frost with icy finger,
   Turned the leaves from green to gold,
Bidding birds not long to linger
   In their Northern nests so cold,
Then across her shoulders shiv'ring,
   Caterpillar skins she'd throw,

Thus protected, without quiv'ring
    She could brave a storm or snow.
Often, down the ice-clad branches,
    While the stars shone, cold and bright,
Swiftly as a vessel launches
    She would glide on wintry night,
But when Spring returned, so blooming,
    Bringing back the birds and flowers,
All her wonted *airs* resuming,
    Sprinkling buds with silv'ry showers,
Then our fairy, sweet and sunny,
    Friends would welcome, old, and new,
Spread for them a feast of honey,
    Drink their health in sparkling dew.
Stories strange the birds related
    Of the lands far, far away,
Till her woodland life she hated,
    And one bright autumnal day,

The Forest Fairy.

With her feathered friends departed
    For their home in Southern clime,
Promising, before she started,
    She'd return by summer time.

Years have passed, and the forest trees
    Have vanished from off the earth,
Some formed the masts to stately ships,
    Or were burned on the glowing hearth.
Where fountains fall, within a park
    The ancient oak is standing, still,
The fairy never has returned,
    Alas! I fear she *never will.*

BABY ASLEEP.

FOLDED the tiny hands,
    As if in prayer,
While myriad angel bands
    Guard the child fair.

Soft swells the fragrant breath,
    Fresh as a rose,
Proving it is not *death*,
    Hushed in repose.

Mark how the rosy flush
    O'er his cheek creeps,
Bright as Aurora's blush,
    Gently! he sleeps.

Then let the zephyrs fan
    His downy nest,
What can be sweeter than
    Baby at rest?

LA MATINÉE DANSANTE.

M ISS ISABELLE Z—
    Is a doll, *tres jolie*,
Three feet is her wonderful height,
    Complexion *bien clair*,
    Chatain doré, her hair,
Her beautiful eyes, brown and bright.

    As she's *really* a Belle,
    I thought I would tell
Of a party she gave not long since,
    It was quite *recherche*,
    And indeed! I might say
Grand enough for a duke or a prince.

She received in pure white,
Which by brilliant gas light
Became her in truth ! *a merveille*,
Her ornaments, pearls ;
Hair, in puffs and long curls,
Skirt *en train* and *corsage, decollette*.

La blonde Violette,
(Mamma's precious pet,)
Made a charming appearance, 'tis true.
She was sweetly arrayed
In a dress that was made
Of black lace, over *Indienne* blue.

Her *coiffure elegante*
Was the taste of her *tante*
But her toilette, her fond grandmamma's.

Miss Lily so fair
With long flaxen hair,
Wore a bright yellow *poult de soie* waist,
With a skirt of *de laine*
Made *en demi train*,
Her dearest friends murmured, what taste!!

A bright *demoiselle*
Was at first quite a belle,
Although she appeared known by none,
Till at last it came out
With an ill suppressed shout,
She was *Suzanne, the children's French bonne!!!*

La Matinée Dansante.

Then there was Miss West
Most gorgeously drest,
In black silk, trimmed with lovely *duchesse*,
Her manners, I know,
Were not quite *comme il faut*
As all by and by will confess.

You will laugh when you hear
The refreshments, I fear,
But the *chef* was a young *amateur*
And 'twas his first *essai*,
So sincerely I pray
Such mistakes not again will occur.

The chief dish was *bouillon*,
Favored by the *haut ton*,
But 'twas made of pink candy and water,

And though good the intent,
One would think the cook meant
The poor dolls' digestions to slaughter.

For 'twas colored with green
As could plainly be seen
Of a bright, intense *arsenic* hue,
And the punch was so strong
That 'twas not very long,
Ere to Charlotte West's head the fumes flew.

And oh ! shocking to tell,
From the sofa she fell,
Then rising, confused all the dancers,
By plunging about,
Now in and now out,
Partnerless in the midst of the Lancers.

A noise in the hall
Interrupted the ball,
'Twas the *chef* who demanded entree,
He had drunk his own punch
By way of a lunch,
And alas! it had made him quite gay.

When Miss West he espied,
He strode to her side,
And requested her hand for the waltz,
Then they capered away,
'Twas as good as a play,
Poor Isabelle called for her salts.

While the butler so stout,
Carried Charlotte West out,
Vowing *punch* she would ne'er touch again.

This broke up the *fete*,
So saying, " 'twas late,"
Each guest made a hasty adieu,
Believe me, my friends
While this history ends
Every word I have told you is true.

THE CORAL TREE.

WHERE sparkling gems and rare,
　　Beneath the blue waves lie,
An insect toils with care,
　　While centuries roll by,
Striving its mission to fulfill
By working out its Master's will.

Slowly, the branching tree
　　O'er ocean's depths doth rise,
Soon, on the broad blue sea
　　A fruitful islet lies,
While brilliant birds and flowers find rest,
Upon its peaceful fragrant breast.

Thus, like the insect small,
  Unwav'ring in its zeal,
Should *we*, with patience toil,
  Constant for *others'* weal,
Sure that the Lord at length will bless,
Our faithful efforts with success.

DEAR SANTA CLAUS.

PERHAPS you'll think it strange that I
should ever dare to write
What I would like for Christmas, but I think
'tis more polite
Than shouting up the chimney, as I've heard
that others do,
I'm almost *sure*, that *you* are of the same opin-
ion too.
You've always pleased me very much, in every-
thing you've brought,
It really seemed as if you knew of what I always
thought,
But lest there should be some mistake, *this* time
I'll write it here

3

And then there need not be upon the subject
     any fear.

I want a pair of pigeons, oh! very much
     indeed!

And please to bring them in a cage, with cups
     all full of seed.

One I would like of snowy white, the other grey
     (I think,)

But both their little eyes and feet must be the
     brightest pink.

About the cage, of course you know which kind
     they will require,

And whether 'twould be better, if 'twere wooden
     or of wire,

Such details I won't mention, as my time 'twould
     only waste,

And you have always proved yourself a *gentle-
     man of taste.*

My sister wants a pretty doll with wardrobe quite complete,

From latest style of bonnet, down to shoes and stockings neat.

As I will have two pigeons, I think I'll give *her* one,

For if she shares them with me, we'll have so much more fun.

Now if you'll only bring them, I'll *very* grateful be,

And prove my thanks by being good, Yours truly, Dickie Z.

A COMICAL COME-DOWN.

ONE bright midsummer afternoon,
    A party sallied forth
In quest of some adventure ;
    Steering their barks due north.

As gayly sailed they onward,
    A cave they did espy,
Perched on a mountain's dizzy height
    That seemed to touch the sky.

Said one, a youth, who did escort
    The gay and errant fair,
"To climb yon steep and towering cliff
    Which one of you will dare ? "

Then out spake all with one accord,
 " Lead on, we each will follow,
Those rocky cliffs we do disdain,
    We'll skim them like a swallow."

The boat is moored, the party starts,
    The brave youth heads the van,
(Clasped in his arms, an infant boy)
    He seemed *almost* a man.

Their dauntless spirits urge them on,
    Although each fair one feels,
It is no joke to clamber up
    Steep mountains, in *French heels.*

Shines down on each devoted head
    The cruel piercing sun,
The earth gives way, the briars rend,
    They find it is no fun.

Now as they faint and fainter grow,
  A dreadful truth doth dawn
Upon each mind, causing them all
  Their luckless fate to mourn.

For—while the placid lake recedes
  Matters are not much mended,
The more they climb, the more they seem
  "'Twixt heaven and earth suspended."

And like an *ignis fatuus*
  The cruel cave doth fly,
For while they climb, it really seems
  Retreating toward the sky.

At last, spoke one, "let's all return,
  For though we climb forever,
We ne'er will reach yon cave though each
  With all her might endeavor."

Now all concurred in this belief
  And all approved the motion,
But *how* they should descend the hill
  They had, alas! no notion.

The gallant youth at length stood forth,
  "Now each shall see," he said,
The question quickly solved, or else
  My name, it isn't Fred."

With his right hand he grasped the child
  And held him high in air,
Then like a deer he bounded down
  The rocks so steep and bare.

Then horror froze the lips of those
  Who did this sight behold,
Ne'er had they seen a deed performed
  So fearful and so bold.

"Come on," there cried a voice below,
　"'Tis nothing when you've done it,
The only trouble now with you
　Is, that you've not begun it."

"He lives," the startled sister shrieked,
　"He lives, I must embrace
The precious babe, alas! I feared
　No more I'd see his face."

Then down the hill she quickly fled
　Love nerved her trembling hands
To grasp the trees to break her fall
　Till on the shore she stands.

To follow her the others strove,
　But ah! they strove in vain,
For coward Fear, with iron grip,
　Their efforts did retain.

" Let's join our hands, and close our eyes,"
    One of the party cried,
" And at a given signal rush
    Adown the mountain side."

" 'Twere better far to perish thus,
    Than cowardly to linger,
And be a mark in future years
    For every scornful finger."

They joined their hands, they closed their eyes,
    Then made one gallant dash,
While 'round them, like the " Light Brigade,"
    They heard a constant crash.

Rocks, roots, and branches, all gave way
    Before this charge so bold,
And downward with a deafening roar
    In swift succession rolled.

Yet paused they not for stock or stone
   In this their mad career,
Nor conscious seem that those they've left
   " Are maddening in the rear."

Fragments of lace, and tresses fair
   Are fluttering in the wind,
From every bush, for all have left
   A *souvenir* behind.

There intervened a thicket dense;
   The hats—oh! where were they?
Ask of the thorns, that ruthlessly
   Have torn them all away.

With sash and scarf and streamer brave
   That well had borne their part,
But the staunchest things that perished there
   Were those *coaching chapeaux* smart.

Yet paused they not for stock or stone
In their mad career.

Breathless, at last they reach the goal,
  Some lame, some bruised and sore,
Gladly they leap into their boats
  And push them from the shore.

And so doth end my story sad,
  The moral's here. beside,
Ne'er boast that you can do a thing,
  Until at least *you've tried*.

THE ORIGIN OF RAIN.

WHEN banished from the garden fair,
    Our parents wound their way,
Oppressed with grief, and worn with care,
    They knelt them down to pray.

Pure angels then, from heaven's height
    The sorrowing ones surveyed,
And weeping vowed, those beings bright,
    They would their efforts aid.

Thus ever hov'ring o'er us all,
    They watch and ward do keep,
And when the pearly rain drops fall,
    Know then—*the angels weep.*

THE FAIRY ISLE.

A FAR on an ocean unknown,
   In a century long gone by,
Where the sun's rays brilliantly shone,
   Nor tempest obscured the sky,
There lay like an emerald rare
   In a setting of pearly foam,
An island enchantingly fair
   Where fairies had made their home.

Oh! from many a distant land
   Had they wandered to this retreat,
Now a loving united band
   Lived they ever in concord sweet.

For the spirits which ruled in the air
　And that guided each elfin mind,
Were Harmony gentle and fair,
　And Justice, firm ever yet kind.

But ah! in each Eden there lurks
　A serpent, and so near the isle
Dwelt a demon whose horrible works
　Were dreaded for many a mile.
His power was great and all knew
　If once he set foot on the shore,
Alas! it was only too true
　That Peace they would know nevermore.

But if they ne'er strayed from the isle,
　Nor turned to his counsels an ear,
Unharmed they securely could smile,
　And know they had nothing to fear,

For Discord was powerless when
   They turned from his presence to fly,
'Twas but when they hearkened that *then*
   Condemned every fairy must die.

One starry summer eve
   When the moon shone clearly down,
The fays their queen did weave
   A flowery dew-decked crown.
And on her pearly brow
   As 'twas placed with loving care,
They sang 'neath leafy bough
   A soft melodious air.

   "Oh! bright as the sun
   Thou beauteous one

Is thy heavenly glance,
  Ah! prithee then smile
  And the hours beguile
As round thee we dance."

Scarce had the words been sung,
  When behold a fearful cry
Throughout the island rung,
  And re-echoed to the sky.
Terror turned each cheek pale,
  And blanched the lips of each fay,
Silence reigned in the vale
  No longer was heard the lay.

Alas! now sounds of strife
  Showed what the shriek portended,
All knew their peaceful life
  Unhappily was ended,

For Discord hovering near
    Had captured some of their band,
And his awful presence so drear
    Pervaded the happy land.

The isle rocked to and fro,
    The moon withdrew her light,
And all was grief and woe,
    Where once it was gay and bright,
Down sank they 'neath the wave,
    While a low mournful wail
Echoed through coral cave,
    Swept by on the passing gale.

Soft zephyrs breathe no more
    In the island bleak and bare,
Fierce winds sweep o'er the shore
    And all is dreary there,

Where Discord dread holds sway
The sun will never smile,
Uncheered by moonlit ray
Is now the fairy isle.

THE BLUE BIRD'S SONG.

I COME from a distant sunny land
   Where zephyrs ever blow,
And flowers bloom, an unbroken band
   Untouched by frost or snow.

Where in forests, *ever* with verdure crowned
   The wild birds chant their lay,
Now in liquid notes, now a joyous round,
   Throughout the livelong day.

Where pendent upon the lofty trees
   Hang fruits, all mellow and sweet,
Which are tossed afar by the laughing breeze,
   To beauteous maidens' feet.

Where brooklets gay wind their onward way,
    With soft melodious flow,
Reflecting the image of every ray
    In dimples that come and go.

But dearly I loved my Northern home,
    Aye, better than words can say,
Although dread winter had bidden me roam
    Full many a long, long day.

So once again in the rippling brook
    I laved my plumage blue,
Then a joyful and long farewell I took
    And back to the North I flew.

Now my heart bounds high with joy to see
    My friends of the year before,
Happy, thrice happy indeed, would I be
    Could I leave them nevermore.

THE WEEK BEFORE CHRISTMAS.

CHRISTMAS is a glorious time,
    Honored oft in prose and rhyme;

But no poet old or young
Praises of the week has sung

That precedes the happy day
Set apart for praise and play.

Too numerous to all narrate
Some of its pleasures I'll relate.

Quickly running to and fro
Through the crowded streets we go;

Now in this store, now in that,
Choosing colors for a mat.

Spending all our precious store,
Wishing that we had *some more.*

Buying toys of every kind
To amuse the infant mind.

Woolly lamb, and life-like cow,
Dogs, that plainly say, " bow-wow."

Talking dolls, and dollies dancing,
Dolls on horses gayly prancing.

Then our parcels home we take,
But with inward fear we quake

Lest some bright inquiring eye
Bundles stray perchance espy.

Faces gay and faces serious,
Open smiles, and smiles mysterious

Greet us now on every side,
Doors no longer open wide.

Every one her needle plies
While each happy hour flies;

Words like these are often heard
From each little sewing-bird.

" Do you think Aunt Mary knows
What I'm making for her, Rose ? "

" Oh ! how pleased dear Charlie 'll be,
When these slippers he will see ! "

Then the dressing of the Tree,
Oh ! delightful mystery !

Box and bundle every size
To bewilder infant eyes;

In the parlor vanish all,
Room forbid to children small.

Expectation on tip-toe
Through the week we gayly go.

And as Christmas Eve draws near
Parents, friends and children dear,

Gleeful girl and boisterous boy
With their hearts brimful of joy,

Cheerily in chorus chime,
" We have had a happy time !"

BONNY BLUE-BELLS.

I N shady nooks
        By running brooks,
Half hid in mossy dells,
        Sweet flowers grow,
        All children know,
The bonny bright blue-bells.

        On mountains high
        Beneath a sky
Of the same azure hue,
        Each year they spring
        And gayly ring,
Those bonny bells so blue.

        When savage storms
        Assail their forms

The wind their death foretells,
　　But though they're small
　　They never fall,
Those bonny brave blue-bells.

　　May they inspire
　　Our souls to higher
Aims than they ever knew,
　　Ere 'tis too late
　　Let's imitate
Those bonny bells so blue.

　　When storms so dread
　　Rage overhead,
And loud the tempest swells,
　　Though children frail
　　We'll never quail
Like bonny brave blue-bells.

THE MIDNIGHT MURDER.

WITHIN a fine farm-yard
    Lived, not long ago,
A hen and three chickens
    With feathers like snow.
They were graceful and pretty,
    And tidy, and neat,
From the crown of their heads
    To the soles of their feet.

To see them together
    In truth was a sight,
In which the good farmer
    Did greatly delight.

No fowl in the farm-yard,
  Would ever molest,
Nor snatch e'en a crumb, from
  This family blest.

Each day they would wander
  In search of their food,
Which often they shared with
  A ravenous brood.
At night in a cottage,
  Securely they'd dream,
Nor wake from their slumbers
  Till morning's first beam.

One evening, while feasting
  On supper of bread,
The youngest chick turned
  To her mother, and said,

The Midnight Murder.

" Don't you think that to-night
  We might roost in that tree?
Oh! if you would let us
  How happy I'd be!"

" You know, my dear daughter,"
  The mother replied,
" No wish of your heart have
  I ever denied.
But although your mind on
  This plan appears bent,
I fear that I really
  Can *never* consent."

" I'm told that fierce creatures
  This region infest,
And we will be safer
  At home in our nest.

Just think! my own darling
    How dreadful 'twould be,
Should an enemy lie
    Concealed in that tree!"

To which the young chicken
    Replied, " It's no use!!!
I see you've been talking
    With that stupid goose.
She's always a story
    Absurd and untrue,
And some silly notion
    Has given to you."

" I'm *sure* there's no danger
    Up there on that bough,
And *I'm* going to sleep there
    To-night, *anyhow*,

Then calling her daughters
Around her she chose
A wide-spreading bough
For their place of repose.

The Midnight Murder.

For if I'm a chicken
    I'm not *chicken-hearted*."
Then off to the tree
    Like lightning she darted.

Of course, the poor mother
    Flew after her child,
'Twixt sorrow and terror
    She almost was wild.
When panting she reached her
    She touchingly said,
" By *your* side is my place,
    Where *you* sleep is my bed."

Then calling her daughters
    Around her, she chose
A wide-spreading bough,
    For their place of repose,

But many an hour
    Passed wearily by,
Ere one of the family
    Closed e'en an eye.

'Twas midnight—and silence
    Reigned over the farm,
And the sleep of the poultry
    Was peaceful and calm.
When—all of a sudden!
    A wild fearful scream
Awakened each sleeper,
    Dissolved every dream.

The farmer's wife quickly
    Rose up in her bed,
" Such shrieks," she exclaimed,
    " Would awaken the dead.

Is that our white hen?
　And where can she be?
The sound seems to come from
　The old apple tree."

" I hope the poor creature
　Has not roosted there,
For a horrid old rat,
　Has made it his lair.
He can't injure *her*
　But her *chickens* he might,
Poor thing! she must be
　In a terrible fright."

Again there resounded
　Throughout the still air,
The poor bereaved mother's
　Shrill shrieks of despair.

4*

Alas! she could do naught
  But loudly bewail,
Her strength 'gainst a fierce *rat's*
  Could nothing prevail.

And so the young chicken
  Was dragged to her fate,
Repenting her conduct
  When it was *too late*.
I trust, my dear children,
  This history may
Prove a warning to those
  Who'd fain disobey.

THE BEAR AND THE BOY.

ON a mountain-top, near a hotel stood
    A bear, which was caught in a neigh-
b'ring wood.
Tied fast to a tree in mild or fierce weather,
He only could move the length of his tether.
Oft silent and sad, he deeply did mourn
When he thought of his friends from whom he'd
    been torn,
And heartily longed once again for a chance
To indulge, as of old in his favorite dance.
As he mused o'er his woes, he made up his
    mind
He'd have his revenge, the first chance he could
    find.

So he bided his time till one luckless day
A little boy came out with Bruin to play.
At first he was timid, and dared not draw near,
Till at length, well assured he had nothing to
    fear,
He went up to Bruin and patted his head,
" Poor bear!   I am *sure* he won't hurt me," he
    said.
Ah! sadly mistaken was our little boy,
And he learned when too late, bears he should
    not annoy.
For straight on his feet Bruin rose from the
    ground,
And with his fore-paws clasped him tightly
    around,
While with a fierce grin, the bear glared in his
    face.
Close and closer became his horrid embrace.

Then loudly, for aid, did our little friend cry,
If not quickly released, he surely would die.
Help happily came, ere he quite lost his breath,
Or he'd really have died a most horrible death.
This teaches us all that we never should dare
No matter how gentle he *seem*, *touch a bear*.

THE BIRD'S FAREWELL.

I N a forest, where the lofty trees
   Adorned with foliage gay,
Were merrily tossed, by the soft breeze
   Afar, in joyous play,
Rung the rich notes of many a bird
   That warbled a blithesome song.
No sweeter notes had ever been heard
   That happy summer long.

For they were singing a long farewell,
   Were bidding an adieu,
To each dancing brook; each mossy dell,
   Ere to the South they flew.

Swallow and blue-bird, linnet and jay,
   The robin and meek dove,
Joined in the carol, that bright, bright day,
   And poured forth sounds of love.

And now they've plumed them for their long
     flight,
   Far to a lovelier land,
While the cheerful rays of the sun shine bright
   On that happy, happy band.
But one remains—'tis the plaintive thrush,
   To sing of their pleasures past,
Just ready to fly from yon low bush,
   She trills *her* song, 'tis the last.

THE LILY AND THE VIOLET.

A LITTLE child one morning strayed
　　Into a garden wide,
And where a fountain blithely played
　　Thither she quickly hied.
Then bending o'er the waters clear
　　She laved her tiny hands,
And watched the fish, now far, now near,
　　Dart o'er the golden sands.

While thus engaged, a gentle voice
　　She heard, distinct though low,
Bidding another to rejoice
　　Whose accents were of woe.

She turned, and in the broad sunlight
  Beheld a violet,
And a lily fair, whose petals white
  With tears of dew were wet.

" Cheer up," the first voice gently said,
  " And drive those tears away,
Droop not so low that lovely head,
  Nor sigh the livelong day."
" Alas!" the lily made reply,
  " I cannot happy be,
So much I fear to fade and die,
  Life has no joys for me!!"

'*Life has no joys!!* oh! Lily dear!
  Say not those words again,
Call not the earth a desert drear
  All full of grief and pain,

Brightly the sun doth shine o'er thee,
  Soft breathes the gentle wind,
The songsters carol joyously
  Of God; so good and kind,
And when at last we fade and fall,
  'Tis as our Maker willed,
Believe; he *will* not us recall
  Till our *mission* be fulfilled."

Abashed; the lily then replied
  " 'Tis as you say, indeed!
I know I should not thus have sighed,
  And will thy counsel heed."
So then her tiny bells so clear
  Gave forth a joyful sound,
While songsters perched on branches near
  Re-echoed it around.

Then lowly bent the little child,
   And with uplifted eye,
In supplicating tones, and mild,
   Thus prayed to God on high:
" Dear Father, grant I ever may
   Attentive prove to thee,
And that I strive, each passing day
   A violet to be."

So may all little children e'er
   Be grateful and content,
Assured that in the end, they'll ne'er
   Have reason to repent.

ALMOST A CATASTROPHE.

OH! listen, children; one and all,
  And a story strange I'll tell
About a cat, that years ago
  In Ireland old did dwell.

A pleasant home our heroine had,
  Her master was gentle and kind,
She dreamed away each sunny day,
  Contented in body and *mind*.
But at last, arose o'er her life
  A cloud of most ominous gloom,
One day she o'erheard him exclaim,
  " For Puss there no longer is room,

Besides she has now grown so old
   She is of no use any more,
Though rats and mice ravage the house
   She never e'en raises a *paw*.
I think that I'll give her away,
   I've a friend who wishes to own
A cat, so I'll generous be,
   And thus 'kill two birds with one stone.'"
The very next day off he walked
   With poor Pussie under his arm.
And gave her away to a man
   Who lived on a neighboring farm.
Then quite relieved homeward he trudged,
   But what was his horror to find
Stretched out by the door as of old
   The cat he had just left behind!!!
" Ha, ha!" he exclaimed, " Mrs. Puss,
   I left you too near your old home,

Next time, I'll take you off farther
 Or backward *again* you may roam."
And so, having made up his mind,
 His plan he matured the next day,
By packing her off to his cousin,
 Whose home was some ten miles away.
That night was his sleep undisturbed
 By dreams of a troublesome cat,
Next morn, he awoke, rubbed his eyes—
 By his bedside, *there Pussie sat.*
She was wet, she was tired, and cold,
 Poor thing!! she had journeyed all night,
I do not believe you e'er saw
 A cat in so sorry a plight;
Enraged, then he loudly exclaimed,
 " You think you may *thus* thwart my will?
I tell you I'm not to be baulked,
 In my head I've another plan still."

So straightway a sack he procured,
   Pushed her in, and sewed her up tight,
The poor thing was quite overcome,
   She *never* was in such a fright.
Then down to the river he ran,
   Threw the sack afar from the shore,
And as he turned backward, he said,
   " *Now* Puss can disturb me no more."
Arrived at his home, he sat down
   In his chair, and quite out of breath,
He began to relate to his wife
   The story of poor Pussie's death,
When all of a sudden! he paused—
   In the midst of the thrilling tale,
For plainly outside of the door,
   He could hear—a *low*, *mournful wail.*
O'ercome with amazement and fear,
   All trembling he went to the door,

Turned the latch, then quickly stepped back,
    For there the *poor drowned cat* he saw.
She was shiv'ring in every limb,
    Wild, hollow, and fierce was her eye,
While undaunted, her mien did maintain
    Do what you *may*, I *will* not die.
Relentless he cried, "ah! I see,
    I forgot to put stones in your sack.
Well! since you've returned without leave
    Just make up your mind to *go back*."
So without any further ado,
    He fills half a sack with *huge stones*,
Then, in spite of her cries, thrusts her in,
    Regardless of feelings or *bones*.
This time, from a very high bridge
    His victim he cruelly threw,
And watched till she sank 'neath the waves,
    Ere from the sad spot, he withdrew.

Now homeward retracing his steps,
   He almost began to regret
His cat, that had proved so attached
   To her home, and had once been his pet.
While musing on her mournful fate,
   Conceive if you *can*, his surprise
To see the cat *race by his side*,
   He scarce could believe his own eyes.
" She ran with wild speed," till she reached
   Once again the beloved old door.
When panting at length *he* came up,
   She was quietly *licking her paw.*
Now as I have stated before,
   He'd already begun to relent,
In his heart of hearts I'm very sure,
   He'd even begun to repent,
But man-like he never would own,
   He ever had been in the wrong.

His sentence he would not revoke,
  Although the temptation was strong.
So quickly, a bag he obtains
  Made of the strongest of leather.
For many years it had withstood
  Alike the wind and the weather.
Then tying it up with a cargo
  Of stones, and his innocent cat,
He said, "I will let you go free,
  If you should escape, after *that.*
To the river thus laden he ran,
  The bag in the midst of it heaves,
The river which seldom gives back,
  What alas! it so often receives.
Then behind the huge trunk of a tree
  All eager he hidden did stand,
Watching, saw Puss arise from the waves,
  And quickly regain the dry land.

Then catching the cat in his arms,
    He vowed that his word he would keep,
And that till she died, 'neath his roof
    In peace, she should *eat, drink*, and *sleep*.
And so he kept true to his word,
    And back to her old home did bring her,
And never *again* turned her out,
    Or into a river did fling her.

THE BOY AND THE BUTTERFLY.

[FROM THE GERMAN.]

(*Boy.*)

"BUTTERFLY, oh little creature!
　　Idly floating in the air,
Tell me how you gain your living,
　What supplies your daily fare?"

.

(*Butterfly.*)

"Breath of flowers
　And bright sunshine,
It is on *these*
I daily dine."

Ardently the wond'ring boy
Longs for such a brilliant toy,
Quickly in pursuit he flies
To secure the precious prize,
But it begs, in tones of woe,
"Darling boy, oh! do not so,
Let me in the sunshine go,
For ere the morning light is shed,
I shall, alas! lie *cold* and *dead*."

THE GYPSY GIRL.

'TWAS in a forest where the trees so green
    Arched over and concealed the varied
  scene
Of ocean, river and of busy town,
And the sun's rays that poured in fury down,

Stood a young maiden who with eager eye
Upward did gaze to the unclouded sky
As if to pierce that deep cerulean dome,
Longing for life beyond; a heavenly home!

Fair were the features of the gypsy girl
'Scaped from its fillet wandered many a curl,

And fell in clusters blacker than the night
Upon a neck as purest parian white.

And straight her form enwrapped in heavy fold
Of crimson cloth, enriched with shining gold,
While from beneath her robe could just be seen
Two tiny feet half hid 'neath mosses green.

But oh! a troubled look this beauteous day
Clouded the face which should have been so gay,
Tears all unbidden, dimmed her brilliant eye,
While to her lip rose the too-frequent sigh.

Now wafted hither by the morning breeze
Which wand'reth sportively amid the trees,
Is heard the ringing tramp of horsemen gay,
As cheerfully they wend their onward way.

Dimly she doth discern, through leafy bough
The foremost of the band advancing now,
Startled, she lendeth an attentive ear,
For these sad words distinctly she can hear,

"Sweetly doth each songster its carol trill,
Softly fall the waters of the sparkling rill,
But, alas! their music cannot joy impart
To a sad existence, and a broken heart."

"For severed from my own, my precious child,
I cannot quell emotions fierce and wild,
Without my darling, all alas! is drear,
E'en Nature faileth my sad soul to cheer."

"Alas! alas! I'll ne'er forget the day
When from my arms my child was torn away,

Ah! when ye stole my daughter, cruel men!
Why killed ye not her wretched father then?"

Upon the gypsy maiden's heart each word
Vibrated tenderly, as 'twere a chord
Of distant music, heard in bygone years,
The mem'ry of which bathed her face in tears.

And hasten, for she droopeth like a reed,
From her bright face, swift doth the blood
    recede,
She's fallen like a statue, cold and still;
Alas! that joy, like sorrow, oft should kill.

'Tis but an instant—she reviveth now,
And wildly presseth with her hands her brow,
Then struggling suddenly upon her feet.
She rusheth forth, the rider quick to greet.

For oh! she seeth once again, a face
Which from her heart, long years could not
    erase,
And cries of rapture through the forest ring,
As from his horse, the rider quick doth spring.

Right joyfully the maid he doth embrace,
While grateful tears adown his bronzed cheek
    chase,
The father with delight is almost wild,
To find the gypsy is his long lost child.

No longer doth the maid in sorrow weep,
No more do visions dark disturb her sleep,
But every day with happiness is rife,
And nothing marreth *now*, the gypsy's life.

THE WELCOME VISITOR.

LONG ago once in Vienna,
  When the earliest morning beam
Touched the turrets and the steeples,
  Bidding sleepers cease to dream,
Walked a man whose noble figure
  Lordlier than his dress did seem.

All absorbed in thought he wandered,
  Noting naught that passed around,
With his mantle wrapped about him,
  And his eyes fixed on the ground,
Planning changes full of import
  Suddenly—he heard a sound.

Looking up, he saw before him
    A sad little figure stand,
'Twas a boy, who blushed and trembled
    Stretching out a timid hand,
Overcome with shame and anguish,
    Charity, he did demand.

Bitter, bitter tears were flowing
    Down the wan and wasted cheek,
Drowning all the light of childhood
    In his blue eyes large and meek.
Touched with pity, thus the stranger
    To the little child did speak.

" You have not the air of others
    Who are used to asking aid,
Will you tell me all your troubles

Little one? be not afraid."
Tenderly he spake unto him,
On his head his hand he laid.

Falteringly the boy then answered,
"You are right dear sir," he said,
"For I was not born a beggar
Poorly clad and illy fed,
Riches once were lavished on me,
But alas! they all are fled."

"My poor father's great misfortunes
And my mother's sickness sore,
Have compelled their child so cherished
Strangers' succor to implore,
But however pressed by famine
I have never *begged* before."

While he spoke the stranger noted
    His refined and noble air,
For his coarse and scanty garments
    Could not hide his beauty rare :
Bending down, he gently murmured,
    " Little friend, do not despair."

" Tell me pray who is thy father?"
    Tearfully the boy replied,
" He was once a wealthy merchant,
    But alas! sir, he relied
On a friend, who stole his money—
    Then he sickened, drooped, and died."

" Sorrows, say they, ne'er come single,
    My poor mother's health declined,
Though she strove to keep it from me,

And she never once repined;
Ah! sir, if you only knew her,
    She's so lovely, good, and kind!"

" But at last her strength has failed her,
    And for many a weary day,
In her wretched bed she's languished,
    While life slowly ebbs away;
In our home so dark and dreary,
    Hope has ceased to shed a ray."

" All last night she moaned in anguish,
    And I feared that ere the morn
Pain and hunger would have killed her,
    So when day began to dawn,
I stole forth to seek assistance
    Ere away she should be torn."

"When I saw you, though a stranger,
　　Something drew me to your side,
Once or twice to speak to others
　　I, alas! had vainly tried,
But your kind and gentle presence
　　Helped me to subdue my pride."

"Ah! have mercy on my mother
　　Or I fear that she will die!"
Sobbed the child; bright tears of pity
　　Gleamed within the stranger's eye.
"Do not weep," said he, "but tell me
　　Does your mother live near by?"

"In the garret of an old house
　　You can see by yonder square."
"And have you not sought a doctor?"

The Welcome Visitor.

"Ah! sir I was going there,
But alas! I cannot pay him,"
"Fear not, that shall be *my* care."

Saying this, he gave some florins
    To the boy, and bade him go
Instantly for a physician,
    To relieve his mother's woe.
Thanking him, the boy sped swiftly,
    Like an arrow from the bow.

Then our hero, unlike others,
    Not content with what he'd done,
Now resolved to see the mother
    Of so lovable a son ;
For the boy's sweet face and manner
    Had his heart completely won.

The Children's Paradise.

Acting quickly on his impulse,
   A few minutes found him there
In the house the boy had shown him,
   Climbing up the shattered stair,
Then the door he softly opened,
   Gently closing it with care.

On this room so poor and barren,
   Poverty had set its seal,
And in every scanty detail
   Plainly did itself reveal,
Failed the " widow's cruse of oil,"
   Empty now " the bag of meal."

Then across the room the stranger,
   Walked with slow and cautious tread,
Toward the scarcely breathing creature

Stretched upon a broken bed.
Horror stricken, low he murmured,
  " Can it be that she is dead?"

At the sound of these soft accents
  Slowly opened the blue eyes,
Resting on the unknown figure
  Languidly, in faint surprise,
Like her son's their hue seemed borrowed
  From the soft Italian skies.

Young in years, but old in anguish
  Seemed the pale and piteous face,
But the high-bred lovely features
  Still retained a winning grace,
Which the heavy hand of sorrow
  Could not totally erase.

O'er her couch, the stranger stooping,
  Murmured kindly words of cheer,
Telling her he was a doctor
  And that now she need not fear,
He could cure her, he was certain,
  Then he dashed away a tear.

Sighing, thus she faintly answered,
  " Useless *now* your healing art,
Death hath warned me, and I feel it,
  Soul and body soon must part,
I am dying, slowly, surely,
  Dying of a broken heart."

" Ah ! think not that I would linger
  On this earth another day,
Gladly would I hail the moment

The Welcome Visitor.

That should bear my soul away,
But my boy! my precious darling!
  For *his* sake I fain would stay."

"Oh! could I but waft him with me,
  From this world of sin and care!
Where the wicked dig their pitfalls
  Youthful footsteps to ensnare,
But to leave him unprotected,
  Fills my soul with dark despair!"

Here, her voice grew faint and broken
  And the stranger turned to hide
His emotion, as he gently
  Begged her in him to confide,
"I'll befriend your boy," he promised,
  "Never fear, whate'er betide."

"But indeed! with God's assistance,
  I will cure you soon," said he,
" And I'll leave you a prescription,
  'Twill relieve you instantly,
Soon from all your pressing troubles
  It will quickly set you free."

While the widow, struck with wonder,
  Thanked him with a grateful look,
Several lines he quickly penciled
  On a leaf torn from a book.
Bidding her to trust in Heaven,
  His departure then he took.

But his bright and cheerful presence
  Had dispersed the heavy gloom,
Which before his happy coming

Overhung the dreary room ;
Death no longer seemed to haunt it,
Like a cold and cheerless tomb.

Scarcely had his parting footfall
    Ceased to echo in the ear,
When the boy returned all breathless
    Crying out, " Oh ! Mother dear,
I have news that will revive you,
    And your wounded spirits cheer."

" God, who from his throne in heaven
    Listens to the raven's cry,
Watches o'er us, and he will not
    Let my darling mother die.
Such a kind, kind friend he sent me
    But I'll tell you by and by ; "

" For the doctor now is coming
    He's but a few steps behind,
When he saw I grew impatient
    Then he said, ' oh, never mind !
Run on, and prepare your mother
    And the way alone I'll find.' "

' Ah ! my son," exclaimed his mother,
    " I have news to tell you too.
As I lay here, faint and lonely,
    Came a doctor, good, and true,
On my heart so bruised and broken,
    Fell his words like healing dew."

" There upon a table lying
    His prescription you will see,
Read it, and perhaps 'twill tell us

What physician he may be.
If I do mistake not greatly
   He is one of high degree."

O'er the lines, the boy glanced quickly,
   Stupefied, began again,
Wond'ring if the morn's adventures
   Had obscured his childish brain,
Till a cry of great amazement
   He no longer could contain.

"What is this I see? my mother,
   Surely I misunderstand,
Ah! pray read it," and the paper
   Thrust he in her trembling hand.
Sorely startled, then the widow
   Rapidly the letter scanned.

6

" 'Tis the emperor, oh, heaven ! "
    Cried she, uttering his name ;
Backward fell she on the pillow,
    While a tremor shook her frame,
Fled the life-tide to its sources,
    Cold as marble she became.

Fortunately the physician
    Now arrived, and soon his skill
Did revive the fainting widow,
    When her eyes began to fill,
Low she murmured, " dear Lord, henceforth
    Bow I blindly to thy will."

" Ah forgive thy sinful servant
    Who against thee did rebel,
Quite forgetting that the future

The Welcome Visitor.

Thou, thou only canst foretell,
Thou who healest all our sorrows,
    Thou, who doest all things well."

" Come, my boy, and kneel beside me,
    Beg the gracious Lord to send
Blessings down on Joseph Second,
    Who the widow did befriend,
And to bless her humble dwelling
    Cheerfully did condescend."

Much the new physician marvelled,
    Scarcely deemed it could be true
That the emperor had been there,
    But his wonder greater grew
When the *magical prescription*
    He had read completely through.

The Children's Paradise.

'Twas an order for some money
   And charge to the account
Of the emperor, and truly
   'Twas no pitiful amount.
Now there is but little left me
   Of my story to recount.

As the widow's sickness only
   Was the fruit of want and woe,
Soon surrounded by life's comforts
   Her recovery was not slow,
And her son rejoiced to see her
   Daily strong and stronger grow.

Every morn, and every evening,
   As the happy grateful pair
Knelt in humble supplication,

Oh! believe that *Joseph* ne'er
Was forgotten, as their voices
　　Mingled in a fervent prayer.

Alms bestowed upon the poor man
　　To the Lord are alway lent,
Joseph ever deemed *his* money
　　Had been well and wisely spent;
Never did he have occasion
　　His kind action to repent.

BERTHA'S BONBONNIÈRE.

'TWAS Christmas-eve, and all Broadway
    Was full of faces beaming
With eager joy, and over all
    A flood of gas-light streaming.

Muffled in furs from head to foot,
    The laughing crowd was striving
Against the icy wind, around
    The corners fiercely driving.

Jack Frost on windows filled with gifts,
    With finger deft traced lightly
Lace patterns, through which shone the goods
    With added lustre brightly.

Bertha's Bonbonnière.

One window more than all the rest
    Attracted much attention,
In truth so gorgeous a display
    Deserves some little mention.

Behind a pane of wondrous size,
    On satin soft reclining,
Delicious fruits from every clime
    In crystal coats were shining.

Bright *bonbonnières* of every hue
    Were grouped in stately splendor,
Suggesting luscious sweets within,
    And mottoes true and tender.

In candied sleigh with tandem deer
    Sat Santa Claus so jolly,
While overhead in gay festoons
    Hung wreaths of Christmas holly.

Amid the gay admiring crowd
  Two figures now advancing
Paused in their progress swift, to view
  This vision so entrancing.

Their well-worn garb with those around
  Ah ! sadly it contrasted,
While pinched and pallid features proved
  Too often they had fasted.

A child of seven the younger seemed,
  Whose tresses long and flowing
About her face the winter wind
  In sportive mood was blowing.

Excitement lent the hue of health
  Until her cheek seemed burning,
Her blue eyes sparkled with delight
  As to the other turning,

I'd like that pretty bonbonnière.

" Oh ! dear Mamma," she gayly cried,
  In accents clear and ringing,
" Just see the toys old Santa Claus
  Behind his sleigh is bringing !

" I never saw such lovely things,
  They make my mouth quite water.
Now don't you think that he can spare
  One for your little daughter ?

" I'd like that pretty *bonbonnière*,
  The white one lined with cherry,
If he would only bring me that,
  'Twould make me happy, very.

" I know I've often heard you say,
  This year he would not visit
Us as he always used to do,
  But, dear Mamma, why is it ?

" I have not been a naughty girl
    But very good, you've told me,
And don't you know that now-a-days
    You never have to scold me ?

" I can't forget the dreadful time
    When we were almost sinking
Far out upon the ocean, and
    It often sets me thinking,

" How thankful I should always be,
    When there were hardly any
Poor little girls that were not drowned,
    Where there had been so many.

" And though Papa we couldn't find
    In this great city cruel,
And oftentimes so very much
    We've wanted food and fuel,

Bertha's Bonbonnière.

"Still, I have tried to do my best,
    Although sometimes I'm fearful
I may have vexed you, when I see
    Your face so sad and tearful."

The mother pressed her darling's hand,
    And answered with emotion,
"Indeed! you never vex me, love,
    So drive away that notion.

"For when you see me looking sad,
    Dear Bertha, it is only
Because I think my little girl
    Must often feel so lonely,

"Far, far away from all her friends
    And her old home so cheerful,
Ah! so unlike our garret drear,
    No wonder that I'm tearful!

"I cannot bear to see you sad,
  And hope you will not sorrow,
Should Santa Claus forget to bring
  You anything to-morrow."

Her little daughter's golden curls
  She smoothed with touch caressing,
While Bertha eagerly replied,
  A secret sigh suppressing,

"Indeed! I'll try hard not to mind
  If Santa Claus forget me,
Why should I care as long as I've
  My own Mamma to pet me."

A smile crept o'er the mother's face
  The mournful lines erasing,
As stooping low, and lovingly
  The little one embracing,

She said, "we'll buy some Christmas greens
  To make the room look cheery,
Come, let us haste, your little feet
  Will soon be growing weary."

"Yes, dear Mamma, I'm ready now,"
  Said Bertha, striving vainly
To hide the tears which in her eyes
  Were shining all too plainly.

Then pausing not once more to view
  The tempting fruit forbidden,
She turned away, and soon they both
  Among the crowd were hidden.

Not long it took to buy the greens,
  Then home they hastened quickly,
For now a blinding storm of snow
  Was falling fast and thickly.

Their wretched room at last they reach
  A garret dark and dreary,
No fire bright to greet them there,
  Chilled through, worn-out and weary.

'Twas midnight, and the little girl
  In bed was soundly sleeping,
The mother, by her darling's side
  A lonely watch was keeping.

Musing on happy hours gone by
  When life was sweet and sunny,
Before she knew how hard it was
  To toil all day for money.

"Yet I could bear it all," thought she
  "With my dear husband near me,
His loving presence would support
  And comfort, aid, and cheer me.

" Oh ! how could I have let him cross
    Alone, the raging water,
And place a barrier between
    His helpless wife and daughter ?

"He deemed it for the best, I know,
    And promised ere we parted
That very soon he'd send for us :
    Then left me broken-hearted.

" For, ever ringing in my ear
    A voice kept on repeating,
' Misfortunes dire will soon transpire
    Perchance there'll be no meeting.'

" Again it came when 'round our forms
    The hungry waves were leaping,
The roar of waters with the words
    A mournful measure keeping.

" But when I felt that hope was o'er
    And clasped my child despairing,
From such a fearful fate we were
    Saved by a sailor daring,

" Oh! then my heart leaped high with joy
    Now, all our woes are over;
Thankful I cried, nor in the sky
    One cloud could I discover.

" Till we had reached this city huge
    And spite of all endeavor,
Could of our loved one find no trace
    But parted seemed forever.

" And now I cannot e'en afford
    A gift for Bertha's stocking;"
Fast fell her tears, when suddenly
    She heard a gentle knocking.

Bertha's Bonbonnière.

Surprised, she hastened to the door,
   And there, upon the landing,
With radiant face, and outstretched arms,
   She saw her husband standing.

No words can paint the meeting glad
   So from the task refraining,
Haste we to listen now while he
His presence is explaining.

"When first the startling news I saw
   About the steamer sinking,
I feared to read the list of deaths
   But like a coward shrinking,

"I waited a few moments more
   But oh! they seemed like ages,
Then glancing down beheld *your names*
   Stand out upon the pages.

" What happened next, I scarcely know,
   My brain was in a fever,
The only words I said were these,
   ' Alas! why did I leave her?'

" Then far away, I journeyed fast
   Nor left one trace behind me,
No wonder darling that you failed
   For weeks and months to find me.

" Some days ago as from a dream
   At last I did awaken
Among kind strangers who had found
   And pity on me taken.

" For many weeks they'd nursed me through
   A fever fierce and wearing,
And ever in my wildest moods
   Were tender and forbearing.

" As soon as I could stand alone,
   To New York back I staggered,
And all to-day have roved the streets,
   A figure, gaunt and haggard.

" To-night as through a window-pane
   I stood, so idly gazing,
Half-hidden by an angle sharp,
   I saw a sight amazing.

" My wife and child whom I had thought
   Beneath the waves had perished,
Again I heard their voices sweet,
   And saw their forms so cherished.

" And while I listened to the tones
   Of Bertha's earnest pleading,
And learned your past and present woes
   My heart was torn and bleeding.

"A quick resolve then shaped itself
  To gratify her longing,
So straightway in the store I went
  Where curious crowds were thronging.

" The prize secured, then with a brow
  From which all clouds were banished,
Triumphantly I stepped outside,
  When lo! your forms had vanished.

" No time I lost in vain regrets,
  But soon found out your traces,
For none who once had seen you both
  Could e'er forget your faces.

"Now let me see my little girl,
  But no—I won't awake her,
I'll wait till morning, then within
  My loving arms I'll take her."

Bertha's Bonbonnière.

Then by the bed-side of their child,
    The happy parents kneeling
Offered a prayer, while down their cheeks
    The thankful tears were stealing.

Next morning brightly shone the sun,
    And through the window peeping
Pried open little Bertha's lids,
    And roused her from her sleeping.

She started up, while half awake,
    And toward the chimney glancing
Her stocking saw, then o'er the floor
    Her feet went gayly dancing.

Pausing before the fire-place
    She saw, oh sight surprising !
The much-desired *bonbonnière*
    From out the stocking rising.

"Oh! Santa Claus is good," she cried,
  "I knew he'd not forget me,
And that he'd never have the heart
  On Christmas day to fret me."

She seized the treasure with both hands
  Then gently raised the cover,
Unconscious of two faces fond
  And eager, bent above her.

And there upon the sweets within
  A card, her vision meeting
Contained these words, "Old Santa Claus
  To Bertha sends a greeting.

"And as he cannot come himself
  Her *Father* acts as porter
To bring a gift she well deserves
  Unto his little daughter."

Bewildered, Bertha raised her head
Thinking her eyes deceived her,
And there beheld her Father's face;
Her Father's arms received her.

THE OLD MAN'S DREAM.

M Y form is bowed with many years, and
sunken is mine eye,

I feel within my inmost soul, erelong that I must
die.

For palsied limbs, and failing strength warn me
my race is run,

Perchance these agéd eyes will ne'er behold
another sun.

Yet sometimes when my spirit is overborne with
care

Sudden, there shines before me, a scene of
beauty rare.

Beneath the lofty shade of a mountain's frown-
ing gaze

There stands my childhood's home where I
passed such happy days.
The sloping roof is covered o'er with mosses
fresh and green,
And 'neath the eaves some swallows' nests quite
plainly can be seen.
Beside the open door-way there stands a spread-
ing beech
Whose topmost bough, though all in vain, I've
oft essayed to reach.
A merry chattering brooklet is running by the
door,
It tells the self-same story that it told long years
before.
I gaze within the window, and there before the
fire
Can see the stooping figure of my venerable
grandsire.

It is the hour of morning prayer, there kneels
    my widowed mother,
One loving arm is thrown around my darling
    baby brother;
Dark robes of mourning clothe her form and a
    tear is in her eye
As she begs the gracious Father from his glori-
    ous throne on high
To look down upon her children in their daily
    walk through life,
And to guard them from all danger, all wicked-
    ness and strife.

A joyous merry shout rings out upon the air,
It is my little sister, who, free from every
    care,
Is running through the garden walks chasing
    the butterfly,

Dancing 'neath the happy sunshine of a cloudless
summer sky;

And now on seeing me she eagerly draws
near

And joyfully cries out, "do you know, oh! Willie
dear

That all the seeds you've planted in the garden
have come up?

They are turning into flowers, so. I picked this
buttercup.

Let me see if you like butter, there! hold your
chin up, so!"

And she eagerly applies the test while standing
on tip-toe.

Then laughing merrily exclaims, "oh dear! you
greedy fellow!

Indeed you *do* like butter, why your chin's a
perfect yellow.

Now come and put me in the swing, and please
    to push me high
Far up among the tree-tops, then—let the old
    cat die."
Smiling, her wishes I obey, then pausing to take
    breath,
Lightly I lean against the tree to witness "pus·
    sie's death!"
Now far o'erhead the darling looks down in
    mimic pride,
Then rapidly descending sweeps swiftly by my
    side.
Her bright blue eyes and rosy cheeks with joy
    and health are beaming,
While unconfined, upon the wind, her golden
    curls are streaming.
In truth it is a spectacle, exceeding fair to see,
This pretty flying picture framed by the apple tree.

Now slowly stroll I onward, till I reach a shady
    dell,
And downward gaze into the depths of an old
    moss-grown well.
The summer wind sighs softly 'mid the branches
    overhead
And whispers wondrous stories of heroes long
    since dead.
Again as in my boyhood bold thoughts I entertain,
While dreams of future glory reanimate my
    brain,
Till the golden summer hours slip all unheeded
    by
And clouds of pink and purple suffuse the
    western sky.

With a start, I awake, 'twas a dream, and 'tis o'er,
I never shall gaze on my childhood's home more,

Every trace of its presence has vanished, I
know.
Consigned to oblivion, long, long ago,
On the forms that I cherished so fondly, of old,
Cruel Death hath long since laid his impress so
cold,
Yet Faith sooths my spirit and pointing on high
Whispers "mourn not, your loved ones you'll
join in the sky."

CINDERELLA.

Dramatis Personæ.

Cinderella.

Malvina.

Lucretia.

Fairy Godmother.

Prince.

Herald.

Page.

Footman.

Coachman.

Ladies-in-waiting, Courtiers, Pages, etc.

Act I.

Scene I. *represents an apartment with fire-place, beside which is seated* Cinderella, *two sisters reclining in easy chairs.*

Lucretia to Cinderella, (*impatiently.*)
Cinderella, Cinderella, what are you about?
Pile fresh wood on, don't you see, the fire's go-
    ing out?"
Cinderella *hurriedly throws some sticks of
                    wood on fire.*
Malvina, (*angrily.*)
What a smoke you're raising, stupid,

Do you mean to choke us?

Witch-like, you evade our orders

With some hocus-pocus.

Cin., (*imploringly.*)

Ah! indeed, I did not mean it.

Sisters, do not scold me,

For you know that I have always

Done just what you've told me.

Lu.—Stop that whining, take the broom

And sweep this dusty floor.

[*a knock is heard.*

Mal.—Cinderella, Cinderella,

Some one's at the door.

CINDERELLA *drops broom, runs and opens the door, admits page bearing invitations.*

Page (*extending card.*)—

His royal highness invites you all

To come to-night to a full dress ball.

Sisters seize card, exit page, LUCRETIA *dances
around the room and exclaims—*

Oh, dear! oh, dear! what a joy is this;

My heart is overflowing with bliss.

Mal., (clapping hands)—

Oh, dear! I am almost wild with delight

What a glorious time we will have to-night.

Lu. (eagerly)—

Oh! tell me Malvina, pray what will you wear?

Mal.

Why *red* and *pink*, with a wreath in my hair,

And answer me quickly Lucretia dear

In what costume du bal, will *you* appear?

Lu. (consequentially.)

Why my grand brocaded *orange* and *green*

No handsomer dress to-night will be seen!

Mal.

There isn't a doubt we'll outshine them all!

Both (clapping hands.)

Hurrah! hurrah! for the prince's ball!

CINDERELLA *who has all this time been seated by the fire regarding the sisters, exclaims aside mournfully,*

Alas! alas! how I wish *I* could go

'Tis useless to ask ; they'll surely say no.

[*Raising her head she continues,*

Perhaps they're so happy, they may consent,

And their harshness to me for a moment repent.

[*To the sisters.*

Sisters may *I* go to the ball ?

The invitation was for all.

Lu. (holding up her hands in amazement.)

Well this beats all ! now did you ever?

Mal. (emphatically.)

No I never! no I never !

Lu. (indignantly.)

You go to the ball, you ugly creature!

With cinders over every feature!

Mal. (derisively.)

Pray what did you think of wearing, Miss;

Would you go in such a costume as *this?*

[*Points scornfully at* CINDERELLA'S *rags.*

Lu.

You saucy creature, how *dare* you ask?

Go back, and finish your daily task.

[*Exit sisters in great disgust.*

Cinderella (begins to weep and exclaims)—

Alas! alas! how sad is my fate!

I can only be silent and patiently wait.

She raises her eyes pathetically, tableau, curtain falls.

Act II.

Scene II. *represents the dressing-room of the two sisters who are discovered standing in front of two mirrors placed opposite each other, while* Cinderella *is employed in putting the finishing touches to their toilettes.*

Malvina to Cinderella.

Oh! you *stupid, awkward* girl!

How you've made my ringlets curl!

Lu.

Come here and fasten my necklace, quick!

Or I'll strike you surely with this long stick.

[*shakes stick.*

Mal. (peremptorily.)

Come smooth my train, don't you hear me call?
We will *surely* be too late for the ball?

Lu. (holding out necklace)—
Cinderella, here!

Mal. (pointing to her train)—
Cinderella, there!

[CINDERELLA *hesitates, as if uncertain which
way to turn.*

Lu. (angrily)
She really doesn't seem to understand or care!

Mal.
Horrid! awkward! *miserable* dunce!!!

Cin. (tearfully)—
Dear me! I can't do everything at once!

Lu. (impatiently.)
Let's leave her Malvina, oh! come let us go!
For the road it is long, and the horses are slow.

[*Exit Lu.*

Mal.—I'm coming.   [*to Cinderella.*

Now see that you shell all the pease,

Scrub the floor, sift the cinders, get down on

    your knees.   [*forces her down.*

And beg pardon for giving your sisters such

    sorrow,

Then *perhaps* we'll not beat you so hard by to-

    morrow.

    [*Exit* MALVINA. *leaving* CINDERELLA *in tears.*

Cin.

    When will my sorrows ever cease?

    They give me not a moment's peace,

    Oh! how I wish that I could go!

    I would enjoy the dancing so!   [*she weeps.*

Enter fairy godmother, disguised in cap and

gown, CINDERELLA *screams and starts back*

in affright, godmother throws aside cap and

*gown and appears revealed in the dress of a
fairy queen.*

Godm.

> You needn't be the least afraid,
> But dry your tears, my little maid,
> For I'm your godmamma, my dear,
> Come hither your sad heart to cheer.
> I've watched your wicked sisters too,
> Their cruelty they soon shall rue,
> For know that I'm your dearest friend
> And all your sorrows soon will end.
> Now tell me what you want the most
> You'll have it then at any cost.

Cin.   Dear godmamma, I'd like to go
> Unto the ball to-night although
> I have, alas! no evening dress,
> These rags are all that I possess.
>
> > [*Points sorrowfully to her dress.*

Godm.

Fear not, your dress shall be as grand
As any queen's within the land,
But then. my dear, a coach you'll need,
So to the garden haste with speed
And bring a pumpkin lying there
Of golden color, rich and rare.

[*Exit* CINDERELLA *who re-enters with pumpkin
and places it on the floor in view of audience.*

Godm. (*waving wand.*)

Vanish pumpkin, and approach
In thy stead, a gilded coach.

[*Pumpkin disappears and is replaced by
coach.*

Godm. Bring the mouse-trap, quickly now,
For we've not much time, I trow.

[*Exit* CINDERELLA, *re-enter with trap, places it on
floor.*

Godm. (*waving wand.*)
　　Disappear, ye tiny mice,
　　Come back ponies, in a trice!
[*Trap disappears, enter ponies led by a
　　　　groom,*
Godm.　Look behind the cellar door,
　　Half concealed upon the floor
There a rat-trap you will find,
A huge rat within (*Cinderella starts*) don't mind
　　You have nothing *now* to fear
　　Bring it hither, daughter dear."
[*Exit* CINDERELLA, *re-enter with trap, which she
holds at arms' length, then places carefully
on the floor.*
Godm.　Vanish rat-trap, come instead,
　　Coachman with a powdered head.
　　　[*Trap disappears, enter coachman.*

Godm.   Close beside the apple tree
           There a lizard you will see,
           Bring it hither with all speed
           For of that too, we'll have need.

[*Exit* CINDERELLA, *re-enter with watering-pot
           containing lizard.*

Godm. (*waving wand.*)
           Disappear, oh! lizard small
           But return, a footman tall.

[*Watering-pot disappears, enter footman.*

Godm.

And now my dear, your dress I'll change
For certainly it would seem strange
Should you appear in such a guise
To-night before the prince's eyes.

[GODM. *waves wand when* CINDERELLA'S *shabby
    dress vanishes and is replaced by an elegant
    court costume, she still retains her old shoes.*

Godm.

    For each foot here's a crystal shoe

    And *now*, my dear, I think you'll do.

                [*approvingly.*

[GODMOTHER *presents* CINDERELLA *with shoes*

    which she hastens to don.

Cin.   O! *thank* you, dearest godmamma,

    You are too good to me, by far.

Godm.

  My kindness you deserve, my child,

  For you were ever good and mild,

  But mind what I've to say, my dear,

  For should you disobey, I fear,

  'Twould vex you greatly, so take care

  To leave at *twelve o'clock*, nor dare

  To stay a *second* longer, or

  You'll wish to sink beneath the floor,

  For ah! 'twould give you great distress

To see old rags replace this dress.
Your gilded coach and retinue
Would likewise vanish quickly too.
And in their stead there would be found
Rat, lizard, mice, and pumpkin round.
Come, to the palace now repair
'Tis fully time that you were there.

[GODMOTHER *leads* CINDERELLA *to the coach the footman assists her to enter, then takes his place beside the coachman on the box, coachman cracks whip,* CINDERELLA *leans forward and smilingly waves an adieu ; curtain falls.*

Act III.

Scene III. *represents a ball-room in the royal palace, the prince is seated on a throne at the head of the room, band plays a march, knights and ladies promenade, the music ceases suddenly, enter* Cinderella, *promenaders pause and gaze at her with mingled curiosity and admiration, the prince starts up exclaiming,*

Prince.

Heavens! what an exquisitely beautiful face!
What a marvellous figure! what wonderful
    grace!
[Cinderella *advances to the foot of the throne
    with dignity, curtesies low, and says,*

Cin.

Great prince! your gracious pardon I request
For coming here an uninvited guest.

[*The prince descends from the throne, takes her
hand, kisses it with gallantry and replies.*
Prince.

Mine is the obligation, beauty bright!
Accept my thanks for coming here to-night.

[*Aside.*

She must be a duchess, or princess, or queen,
Ne'er saw I before a statelier mien.

[*To Cin.*

Sweet lady, may I now demand
For the next dance, this beauteous hand?

[Cinderella *bows assent, the band strikes up the
Lancers, the set forms and dances. In the
midst of the grand chain, the clock strikes
twelve,* Cinderella *at first does not appear*

to hear, then frightened attempts to withdraw, the prince endeavors to detain her, but
she breaks away forcibly just at the concluding stroke, dropping her slipper, the prince
seizes it, presses it to his lips and exclaims,
Prince.

My courtiers, seek her far and wide
For *she alone* shall be my bride.
[*Consternation among the ladies, who all raise
their handkerchiefs to their eyes ; grand tableau—curtain falls.*

Act IV.

Scene IV. *The sisters and* Cinderella *are discovered at home, the sisters lounging in easy chairs,* Cinderella *bending over some sewing; as the curtain rises the work drops from her hand and she appears absorbed in a revery.*

Mal. to Cin.

You careless creature, attend to your work!

Lu.

She's *always* trying her duty to shirk!

Mal.

Oh! wasn't the ball a grand affair?

Lu. to Cin. (tauntingly)

Ah! don't you wish that *you'd* been there?

Mal.

I think of the princess night and day,

Where do you think she came from, pray?

Lu.

Do you know, when she entered the palace door

It seemed to me I had seen her before?

Cinderella, (aside tremblingly.)

Ah! should they discover me what would they

do?

I believe they would *hang* me, and *quarter* me too,

That would be a fit end to my miserable fate,

Oh! *why* was I tempted to linger so late?

[*Enter herald bearing proclamation, he reads*

aloud.

Herald.

Know then ye ladies, great and small,

Whoe'er was at the princess' ball

His highness has made up his mind

The owner of this shoe to find (*produces shoe*)
And whom the slipper fits, why he
Will marry then most certainly.

  Mal. (*impatiently.*)

      Pray let my have the shoe, for it
      My slender foot will surely fit!

  Lu. (*dictatorially.*)

      Malvina, let *me* have it first
      That slipper, *you* will surely burst!

  Mal.

      For shame! how can you be so mean?
      Perhaps *you'd* like to be the queen?

  Lu. Pray why not *I*, as well as *you?*

      Do you not hear? hand me the shoe!

[*They struggle violently for the slipper, at last*
MALVINA *succeeds in securing it and endeav-*
ors to force it on her foot, the others look on
eagerly and anxiously.

Mal. (tugging away.)

It's going on! (*mournfully*) oh, no! oh, no!

It's all the fault of that *great toe!*

> [*strikes foot angrily.*

Lu. (sneeringly.)

Didn't I tell you so? my love,

Hand me the shoe, my *precious dove!*

[MAL. *throws shoe at her sister and begins to sob.* LUCRETIA *strains away vigorously at putting on the slipper.*

Herald.

How red she's getting in the face!

We'll have to cut her corset lace!

Mal. (spitefully.)

She'll have an apoplectic fit, I fear,

Hadn't you better give it up, my dear?

Lu. (triumphantly.) It's on!

Herald and *Mal.* It's on?

Cin. Alas! how I feel!

Lu. (sorrowfully.)

    All but the heel!

Herald and *Mal. (laughing.)*

    All but the heel!

Lu. (desperately.)

    I'll cut it off! hand me a knife!

    For I *will* be the prince's wife!

Herald. (advances, wrests the slipper from

        Lu *and says,)*

    That question Madam, *I'll* decide,

    For you are not the rightful bride,

    And now I will pursue my way

    Wishing you all a pleasant day.

[HERALD *bows and is about to withdraw, when*
CINDERELLA *advances with dignity and ad-
dresses* **him** *modestly but firmly.*

Cin.

My friend, you have almost forgotten, I fear,

That another lady was also here,

But without making any further ado .

Will you be so kind as to hand me the shoe?

Herald. (with confusion.)

Certainly, Madam, I did not see,

[*he kneels.*

And I crave your pardon, on bended knee.

[*Aside.*

Although she is clothed in a ragged old dress

Her manners are *regal*, nevertheless!

[*The sisters hold up their hands in mute amaze-
    ment, while* CINDERELLA *calmly proceeds to try
    on the slipper, which goes on readily. She
    then takes the mate from her pocket and puts
    it on her foot, in the meantime, the fairy god-*

mother enters, touches Cin. *with wand and transforms her into the princess of the ball.*

Sisters, (*with clasped hands.*)

 Can I, can I believe my eyes!

Herald.

 It was the princess in disguise!!!

Godm. to *Cin.*

My pretty godchild, I have come to see

Your triumph over such vile cruelty.

Your shameless sisters, I condemn to stand

Beside your royal throne, on either hand,

To witness all your glory and your power,

And suffer torture daily, hour by hour,

No punishment so great to them, I ween,

As to behold their injured sister, *queen.*

A lesson this to tyrants should afford,

Know, Virtue always meets its just reward.

Curtain falls.

The concluding tableau represents the state apartment of the palace; the prince and CINDERELLA are seated upon a throne, on either side of which stand the two sisters with averted glances of envy and hate; ladies-in-waiting, courtiers, pages, etc., complete the picture.

www.ingramcontent.com/pod-product-compliance
Lightning Source LLC
Chambersburg PA
CBHW030601040726
47497CB00008B/2821